Zapped out

I HAVE LEARNED SOMETHING NEW HARRY. WOULD YOU LIKE TO SEE IT?

WHAT IS IT?

WATCH

I said, "I'm watching. Do your stuff."

The computer disappeared. I mean the sucker completely vanished. It totally zapped out and disappeared. Nothing was left.

"Nice trick," I said to myself, I guess, now that I was alone.

**Other Apple paperbacks
you will enjoy**

Our Man Weston
   by Gordon Korman
Blaze
   by Robert Somerlott
Frank and Stein and Me
   by Kin Platt
Two-Minute Mysteries
   by Donald J. Sobol
The Sick of Being Sick Book
   by Jovial Bob Stine & Jane Stine

THE COMPUTER THAT ATE MY BROTHER

DEAN MARNEY

AN
APPLE
PAPERBACK

SCHOLASTIC INC.
New York Toronto London Auckland Sydney

For Dylan

ISBN 0-590-44005-5

Copyright © 1985 by Dean Marney. All rights reserved. Published by Scholastic Inc., 730 Broadway, New York, NY 10003, by arrangement with Houghton Mifflin Company. APPLE PAPERBACKS is a registered trademark of Scholastic Inc.

12 11 10 9 8 7 6 5   3 4 5/9

Printed in the U.S.A.   01

First Scholastic Printing, March 1987

One

This story is about my brother and about a computer I once knew. The computer isn't here anymore. (I have wished I could say the same about my brother.) I don't know exactly where it is now and I've never known another one like it. To tell you the truth, if it still exists I'm not sure it could really be called a computer anymore.

I keep thinking that one of these days I'll wake up in the morning and there it will be — just like this dog that used to show up on our porch every once in a while. I'd try to keep him and make him mine, but he would only hang around for a while and then he'd disappear. I'd look for him for a few days but then I'd give up, thinking he'd probably been poisoned, or run over, or had moved in with someone else.

Then he'd show up, hungry as anything, acting like nothing had happened. I keep thinking maybe the computer will be like that dog. Except the dog finally stopped showing up.

I met the computer on my twelfth birthday. That morning at breakfast, my mother had said that twelve was a magic year.

"Twelve is magic. It's solid. Not like fifteen is solid, but solid nevertheless. Thirteen can be a bad-luck year but only good things can happen when you're twelve." My mother had said this while putting French toast on my plate. She told me she had made French toast because it was my favorite.

French toast is my brother Roger's favorite. I hate French toast. Roger is fifteen, and if that makes him more solid than I am, it's a joke.

My mother said, "Now remember, we're going to celebrate your birthday properly tonight at dinner!"

I could hardly wait. Dinner, however, turned out to be no big deal. No one else would even have known it was my birthday if you hadn't told them. I mean, we didn't wear party hats or have balloons or anything. The only way a stranger would have known that I was having a birthday was that after dinner my mother brought in a cake. Everyone sang except Roger, who was hollering, "Happy birthday to you. Happy birthday to you. Happy birthday, dear Bozo, happy birthday to you."

I looked at the cake.

"Twelve candles," my mother said. "Twelve is such a wonderful, magic age."

"Blow out the candles," Roger said. "They're dripping wax on the cake."

"I have to think of a wish first," I insisted. I was feeling stubborn.

My mother said, "Thirteen can be a bad-luck year but only good things can happen when you're twelve."

I closed my eyes and tried to think of a wish fast. I thought, Wish to be invisible. Wish to be carried away in a flying saucer. Wish to be a rock star.

My mom handed me a knife and said, "Why don't you cut your cake, Harry?"

My little sister, Joanie, blurted out, "I'm not having any because Roger spit on it twice while you were blowing out the candles."

Roger started laughing, adding little snorts like a pig coughing. He looked at Joanie and stuck two fingers first into the cake and then into his mouth. "Pretty good," he said.

"Really, Roger," my mother said.

He ignored her. "I've always wanted to do that," he said. He then changed the sound he was making to the kind of laugh that chain-saw murderers commonly use, went upstairs, got his jacket, and left the house. My dad yelled as Roger slammed the door, "Where do you think you're going?"

The room was silent. I finally cut myself a piece of cake, avoiding the part where Roger stuck his fingers into it, and took a bite. It was pretty good.

"Now let's have a happy birthday," my dad said cutting himself a huge piece of cake.

Joanie asked to be excused. "NO," my mother said.

They let Roger ruin everything as usual, I thought to myself.

"How about a present?" My dad was trying to save the occasion. He led me over to the corner of our living room where a very large package sat with a green bow on it.

"Well, go ahead and open it," my mother said.

I carefully lifted the bow and slowly began stripping off the paper. Joanie got impatient and helped me. We got it unwrapped and there it was — a plain brown box.

"Just what I wanted," I said.

My dad laughed. "Look inside," he said. "The suspense is killing me."

I looked inside.

"It's a TV," I said.

My dad was grinning like Ronald McDonald. "It's not," he said.

I suddenly realized what it was. It was a computer.

"You're kidding," I said.

"Now, it's an investment in your future," my dad said, "and I have to be honest and tell you that I got it secondhand, but the woman who used it before was a grandmother and a retired math teacher. The shop said it might as well be new. They figured she probably never even used it."

"But, still," I said.

"I know it's what you always wanted."

It wasn't. Not that I wasn't grateful. It was a great gift. But what I've really always wanted is a drum set.

"Well, thank you very much," I said.

We stood around smiling at each other for a few minutes.

"Maybe I should set it up," I said finally.

"Let me help you carry this up to your room and we'll set it up there," Dad said.

"Okay," I answered.

Joanie took some frosting off my collar and stuck it in her mouth.

Upstairs, while my dad was getting everything ready, I excused myself and went into the bathroom. I looked at myself in the mirror.

"Happy birthday, Harry," I said and tried to lick a coating of sugar off my nose.

Through the doorway I could see Dad in my room, plugging in the computer. As he turned it on, a message appeared on the screen.

HAPPY BIRTHDAY HARRY

"Now isn't that something," I could hear my dad say. "How did they make it do that without my even telling them what your name is?"

Two.

I would do almost anything to have some sort of control over Roger. He's three years older than I am and about twenty pounds heavier so I can just forget it, but there is one thing that you should know about him: Roger is the worst possible slime ever to walk on the face of this earth, and if he touches my new computer, I swear I'll do something he'll regret.

Dad was so pleased with himself for getting me a computer, I couldn't believe it. He was beside himself. After I washed my face and changed my shirt, I went into my room where he showed me the screen that said HAPPY BIRTHDAY HARRY. He jumped up and down as much as someone who is at least fifty pounds overweight can jump.

"Isn't that something," Dad said. "It was on

the screen like that when I turned it on. The guy at the shop must have done it before he packed the machine up."

I was trying to figure out how the man could have done it and how I could erase it from the computer so the screen wouldn't flash HAPPY BIRTHDAY HARRY every time I turned the power on, when suddenly the words started to form into a big ball that bounced up and down a couple of times and then bounced off the screen.

Joanie said, "Wow, we are talking weird."

The remarkable thing was that there was no disk in the disk drive and no one had touched a key yet. Now the screen was blank. I shut the machine off, put in a games disk my dad had gotten as a freebie with the computer, and turned the computer back on.

Everything worked the way it should have. The games were only so-so and playing them with Joanie and my dad made them even more so-so. I didn't let on about my true feelings, though. Since it was my birthday I laughed and acted really happy so my dad could feel good about giving me a computer.

After a while I said I was beat and should probably go to bed. Mom came into the room and told Joanie that she would be exhausted to-morrow if she didn't get to sleep soon so I turned off the computer and we all went to bed. Of course that didn't include Roger, who wasn't home yet.

I fell asleep quickly but something woke me up. I looked at the clock on my nightstand. It glows in the dark. I'd been asleep less than an hour.

My first thought was that I had been dreaming. I couldn't remember what the dream was about, but it must have been a nightmare. My heart was pumping like I'd just run a race.

Then I heard something. I swear I could hear someone crying. It wasn't like normal crying. It was very high-pitched and sounded almost as though it was coming from inside a box.

I turned on the light next to my bed and looked around the room. I listened again but couldn't hear anything.

I realized then that I was holding my breath. I couldn't move. I have to admit I was scared to death.

Finally, I forced myself to say something. "What's going on?" At the same time I reached for the light and knocked it over.

"Terrific," I said, and I swear on a stack of Bibles that I heard that same sound, now turned to laughter.

Putting the lamp back on the stand I flicked the switch on. The room was empty except for my dresser, my desk, and the computer, which was on it. Everything was just the way I had left it except that it looked like — yes — my computer was on. I could see its light glowing. The trouble is, I knew I'd turned it off. The switch is on the back and it isn't as though you can reach down and turn it off without thinking about it. I distinctly remember reaching back there and turning it off.

Hanging my head over the side of the bed and lifting the bedspread off the floor I checked underneath. "Nothing up my sleeve," I said. I was trying to keep myself cool. It wasn't really working, so I threw back the covers and climbed slowly out of bed. I put on a pair of underwear from the pile of clothes on the floor. (I was trying to get used to sleeping without anything on, thinking it's something that I should learn to do for when I get older.)

Anyway, I didn't want to give whatever it was the impression that I was scared, so I sort of swaggered over to the closet and threw open the door. "I'll murderize ya," I said, intending to make my voice sound really tough, but it came out sounding sort of like Bugs Bunny's. I guess I would have had to murderize a shirt or a pair of pants, anyway. Nobody was in the closet.

I opened the door into the hallway. No sounds were coming from Joanie's room. Someone had probably left the TV on downstairs, but I certainly wasn't about to go down there to make sure. "Actually," I told myself, "it's probably Roger. He probably came home and is gargling or something."

Back in my room I locked the door just to be on the safe side. There was a very remote possibility that the person or thing making the noises was a mass murderer. I then went over to the computer.

"And how did you get yourself turned on?" I said. It beeped. Now I knew for sure I was hearing things. I reached back and turned it off. As I did I could hear it wind down, but it didn't sound right. It sounded like it was heaving a deep sigh.

"Cracker Jacks, Harry. You are definitely Cracker Jacks. Repeat after me: Computers do not cry, laugh, or sigh."

They may not, but I cross my heart and promise to poke a pickle in my ear if I didn't hear my computer do just that. Maybe the thing has a voice synthesizer. Maybe it is one of those talking computers. I couldn't think of what else it could be.

I figured I'd ask my dad in the morning or, if all else failed, I could read the manual.

Three

After breakfast I asked my dad one simple question. I asked him whether he got a voice synthesizer with the computer. He immediately went into this super apology number about how he couldn't afford it. Ten minutes later, when he was through, I of course had to do the same thing, trying to make him feel good by telling him I didn't want a voice synthesizer. I merely wanted to know if the computer *had* one or not

The whole thing was very stupid. First he felt bad. And then, because he wouldn't believe me when I said I didn't want a voice synthesizer, I felt bad. Great. Because of one simple question, two people got to feel rotten and guilty for the rest of the day and probably their whole lives.

Parents think that if you ask them a question, you must want something from them. The only solution is not to ask questions. If every kid learned this simple fact of life, the world would be an easier place to live in. I can predict what will happen: When my dad is on his deathbed, he will turn to me and say, "Harry, I'm sorry I didn't get you a voice synthesizer."

I will say, "But I didn't want a voice synthesizer."

Dad will say, "I know you really did and that's why it is so nice of you to say you didn't want one. I've been an awful father."

Then he will die and everything bad that happens in the world will be my fault. Sometimes I wonder if my life would be a whole lot better if I never said a word.

Roger never feels bad or guilty about anything. How can you, if you don't have a heart? How can you, when you think only about yourself twenty-four hours a day? How can you, when you throw up outside someone's door and don't clean it up?

It happened last night. Roger decided to stumble in after we had all gone to bed and had been asleep for a while. I looked at the clock. It said 3:00 A.M. Roger had crawled up the stairs and made it to my door before he blew his chips. I couldn't believe it! Of course I just stayed in bed and tried to pretend it hadn't happened. Before I could even get downstairs to eat breakfast the next morning, however, I had to help my mother clean up the floor. I just want it on the record that this is not the way to start your day.

My mother said, "Roger must have the flu."

"Yeah, and I'm Santa Claus," I wanted to say.

I finished my breakfast without mentioning the computer. I had decided to forget it. Maybe I had been walking in my sleep or something last night. Maybe I dreamed the whole thing. A computer obviously can't make humanlike noises. It just can't. It can ring its bell, which really sounds like a beep, but it cannot sound like a human. And whatever was making those noises last night sounded human.

After breakfast, when I went up to my room to grab my coat, I noticed the computer was on again. I screamed at Joanie. "I don't care if you use my computer, but you have to shut it off when you're through."

"I didn't touch it," said Joanie.

I yelled at Roger, "Keep your greasy fingers off my computer."

Roger was in the shower and didn't hear me.

I shut the computer off and went to school. It didn't make any strange noises when I flipped the switch, but I checked it twice to make sure it was off.

School was okay that day. This girl I know — her name is Amy — kept saying "Hi" to me between classes. She could have gotten on my nerves except I kind of like her.

After school I ran home. I usually walk but today I was thinking about getting in shape. Once I was home though, I forgot about getting in shape and devoured three doughnuts I found in the kitchen. I grabbed a glass of milk and went upstairs to play with my birthday present.

The darn thing was on again. This was beginning to drive me crazy.

"What is going on?" I said to the air.

The computer just hummed.

"Is this thing haunted?" I was kidding.

The computer hummed a little higher.

I shut it off again and changed my clothes. My back was to the computer when I suddenly had an odd feeling that I was being watched. I whipped around. The light on the keyboard was shining. Someone or something had just turned it on.

I checked my room and yelled out in the hallway, "Is anyone else here?"

There was no answer. My mom and dad were still at work and this was Joanie's day for her piano lesson. Roger was probably lying in some gutter somewhere.

"Okay," I said to myself, "the house is haunted but at least the ghost is a pretty harmless one. It only turns on computers. Weird, though, very weird."

I considered leaving the house right then but I somehow sensed that nothing was trying to hurt me. Don't ask me why. I just knew that. Things were definitely weird but they were safe.

So I turned on my radio to keep me company. When I was five my baby sitter told me that radios kept ghosts away. That is when I made my parents buy me one.

With nothing else to do, I sat down at the computer and put a games disk in the disk drive. I tried to boot it but I kept getting an error message and then the screen flashed RETRY. It was refusing to boot the disk. I retried all six of my games disks. Nothing worked.

Finally I put a blank disk in. I thought maybe I could initial it, and it would let me do a little programming, something simple. I slipped in the disk and immediately the computer let out an "ahhhhhhhhh."

I jumped a little. Actually I jumped a lot. I tried to give the computer commands to initial the disk but no matter what I did, I couldn't get it to accept a command.

The light on the disk drive was glowing now. The word BUSY was on its screen and wouldn't budge. I could hear it writing something on the disk. I assumed it was writing and not reading because the disk was blank.

The problem was that I couldn't figure out how or why it was doing this. "With my luck," I said, "it's probably broken."

After about five minutes the light went off on the disk drive. Whatever it had been doing was done. The computer was just sitting there looking at me, humming in a way that sounded happy, if you can imagine that. I tried to reach around and turn it off in case it was going to short out or something, but when I put my finger next to the switch, the computer let out this really angry beep.

It sounds peculiar, I know, but with this machine you've really got to know your beeps. Stepping back a minute to consider what I should do, I thought about calling my dad, but he probably wouldn't know what to do either. I tried looking in the manual but finally gave up. I wondered if I'd hurt it by unplugging it.

Before I could decide what to do next, this song I like came on the radio. So I turned up the volume.

The song had an excellent beat, with these super keyboard riffs. I don't know the title but it's about love and stuff and it made me think of Amy. I was really starting to get with it, dancing and pretending to do the keyboards on my dresser, when I glanced over at the computer. The screen was totally freaking out.

It was flashing characters so that one minute the screen was all black and then the next minute it was all white.

"Cripes," I said, "now what do I do?"

I went for the plug. The letters stopped jumping around and began to form words.

HARRY DON'T UNPLUG ME.

I unplugged it immediately. Hey, I'm not crazy. I didn't want to get involved with a haunted computer.

I am not the type of person you see all the time in horror movies, who goes to check out the noise in the cellar or who sees blood dripping down a wall and goes upstairs to see what's there. It isn't that I'm a chicken. I'm just smart. In my book, when you're dealing with something that has the potential to hurt you or freak you out, the policy to follow is "Leave it alone."

I calmly jumped down the stairs, four at a time, ran outside, and slammed the front door behind me. It seemed like a good idea to go to the library until dinner. That would impress the folks, I thought. Besides, it has comfortable chairs and the books can be pretty good sometimes.

When I got there, I found both a good book and a place to sit down but I couldn't concentrate. I kept saying over and over to myself, "the computer knows my name. It isn't supposed to know those things."

The librarian, Jeff, who's a pretty cool guy, came over after a while and told me that it was closing time. In our town, they always close the library for an hour at dinnertime.

I went home, prepared to talk to my dad about getting the computer repaired.

"Roger, is that you?" my mother said as I came in the door.

"No," I answered, "it's just me, Harry."

"Oh, Harry, we're having your favorite for dinner. Meatloaf!"

"It's Dad's favorite," I said.

She said, "Harry, when I came home your radio was blaring away so loud I couldn't hear myself think. Did you leave it on all day like that? It's a wonder that the neighbors haven't complained. Or if they tried to complain we never heard them."

I started to explain but she told me to go outside and see if I could find Roger. As I went out the door I said, "I'll look under the nearest rock."

Four

At dinner Joanie asked me what I had done to my computer. I almost blew meatloaf out my nose before I could answer.

"What do you mean?" I barked. "What were you doing fooling around in my room with my computer?"

"Well, I wasn't fooling around with it. I couldn't," she said. "Every time I tried to do anything, it would ask me where Harry was."

"Now how did you do that, Harry?" my dad asked.

"Oh, it was no big thing," I said.

Roger made his entrance just then. I sat there and thought how good he'd be in one of those horror movies where the guy is crazy and runs around killing everyone. It isn't that he looks like a monster. In fact he's actually the opposite. He's a lot better looking than I'll ever be. I mean he practically started shaving in the third grade. I'll probably never have to shave. And he's got muscles even though he never works out.

But he's cruel. You can tell just by looking into his eyes. He has eyes that look right through you, as if you're not even there.

When we were little and we walked to school together, he'd push me into any mud puddle we passed. He'd never say anything, he just did it.

"Here, Roger," my mother said. "I made your favorite."

Roger just looked at her and then dished up his plate.

"How was school today, Roger?" Dad asked.

"Couldn't be better," said Roger without lifting his head.

My dad went on to tell us about some article he was reading or had read. I don't remember which because I wasn't really listening. No one else was either. I don't even think my mother was listening. Roger certainly wasn't. He was chomping down the food like there was no tomorrow.

I did remain alert enough to hear Dad say

something about kids today and peer pressure and the stress of living in a drug culture. I wanted to tell him to just come out with it. I wanted him to say, "Roger, if you're using drugs I'm going to have to do something drastic."

I wondered if Roger really hated us as much as he seemed to. I know it's sick, but a part of me somewhere deep inside wanted Roger to like me. It sounds crazy, but I can think of one or two times in my life when I almost got along with him.

After dinner I went upstairs to tackle the computer. Joanie followed me. "Can't a person have any privacy in this house?" I said.

"Excuse me!" Joanie whined. "I just wanted to watch you play with your computer."

"I'm not going to play with my computer," I lied.

"Well then, can I play with it?"

"Forget it," I said. "Get your own computer."

"I'd like to," said Joanie.

I knew I'd hurt her feelings so I said, "Come back in about an hour and I'll let you play with it then. I've got some homework to do right now."

That must have satisfied her because she went off to watch TV. I was alone — sort of.

Roger was in his room, which is right next to mine, blasting his stereo. That's great. I get in trouble for playing a radio a little loud but Roger can make the walls vibrate and it's okay.

My dad came all the way upstairs to Roger's room. He knocked on the door and said, "Roger, could we turn it down a little?"

It was a nice try but it didn't do any good. Roger had his door locked and he probably couldn't hear Dad because the music was so loud.

Well, you've probably guessed it. I went over to my computer and, to my surprise — ha! — the dumb thing was on. That idiot machine is going to cost us a fortune in electricity. I sat down and put in the disk the computer had written after school. Then I turned the machine off and then back on again to boot the disk. The cursor appeared on the screen.

I typed CATALOG.

Now I expected to see a list of programs come up on the screen. That's what a person would expect of any ordinary computer. I thought at the very least I'd get some sort of error message. Silly me. I guess I should have expected anything but the norm from this machine.

The screen read HIT SPACE BAR TO CONTINUE.

"Continue what?" I said under my breath.

Just then my dad stuck his head in my door.

"How can you hear yourself think with that racket in the next room?" he said.

"It isn't easy," I replied.

"What are you doing?"

"Oh, just goofing around."

He came over and looked at the screen. "Well, are you going to continue?" my dad asked, grinning. I couldn't believe how into this whole computer business he was. He should have bought the machine for himself. I probably would have been better off.

I hit the space bar and the message on the screen read: HARRY IS THAT YOU? Y/N?

I assumed that Y meant *yes* and the N meant *no*. I typed in Y and hit the return.

"Is this something you programmed?" Dad asked me.

"Sort of," I said. I wished I could get rid of him.

HELLO HARRY the screen read.

At this point I was trying to act as if I knew

what I was doing. My dad started asking me how I programmed it, and I told him these incredible lies. I didn't know what to do. I couldn't tell him it was a program the computer wrote by itself.

"Well, that's about all I did," I said.

"What happens when you type in HELLO back?"

"Oh nothing," I said.

"Give it a try?"

"Dad, it's just a machine. It only does what you program it to do. It doesn't create things. I'll show you."

I typed in HELLO.

The screen read HELLO AGAIN HARRY. IT IS GOOD THAT YOU ARE FINALLY TALKING TO ME THIS WAY. PRESS THE SPACE BAR TO CONTINUE.

My dad said, "You kidder you. You're so modest."

What could I do? I pressed the space bar. On the screen appeared the number 5.

"Well, that's definitely all I had time to do," I said, "so come back a little later and I'll show you how I'm going to finish it up."

"Oh, let me watch," Dad said.

Mom saved the day by yelling up the stairs,

"Walt, the washing machine is leaking again."

My dad said, "Goodness grief," which is the way he swears. "I guess I'll have to come back later."

He left the room, muttering something about it being time they stopped messing around with that old machine and got a new one. They won't though. The machine is one that my great aunt Eudora bought four years ago, just before she died, and left to my mom. Mom is just nuts about keeping things that dead people give her. You wouldn't believe some of the junk she keeps just because someone died and left it to her. We are talking about a collection of the ugliest salt and pepper shakers that were ever made. My dad just nods his head and says, "If it's important to you."

I got back to the computer. I had no idea what 5 was supposed to represent so I asked it: 5?

The screen came back with HARRY YOU HAVE 5.

Five what?" I thought.

5? I typed in again.

The computer came back with HARRY YOU HAVE 5. HOW MANY DO I HAVE?

5 WHAT? I asked again.

It started beeping and making that sound that reminded me of crying. Now I knew for sure I hadn't been dreaming last night. The computer was definitely crying.

Quickly I typed in PLEASE STOP CRYING. I CAN'T TAKE IT.

The computer stopped crying.

I sat and thought, What do I have five of? I typed in TOES?

There was no response.

I tried TOES? again.

The screen replied YOU SAID THAT.

"Sorry," I said.

I tried FINGERS?

There was no response again.

I couldn't think of any more fives except five men on a basketball team or five days of school in a week. It just couldn't have been those.

"What are some other things that are five?" I said aloud.

The computer beeped and on the screen appeared HARRY YOU HAVE 5 SENSES. HOW MANY DO I HAVE?

What are the five senses? I thought. Well there's taste for one. (Naturally I thought of food first.) Now let me see, there's also sight and, of course, hearing. That makes three.

Smelling! I could do without that sense when I'm around Roger. In fact I could do without all the senses when I'm around Roger.

What was the last sense? The five senses are: Sight, smell, hearing, taste, and . . . I couldn't think of the last one. Let me see, if I found something new, really discovered something and I had to describe it to someone, how would I go about doing it?

I could describe what it smelled like. I could say what it tasted like. (I would have to be extra careful with that one. I mean, what if I had just discovered dog poop?) I could tell what it looked like and I could also tell if it made a noise or not. I could tell if it was smooth or rough.

That's it! The fifth sense is touch. Whew! That was hard work.

Okay, so I have five senses and I know what they are. I typed on the computer YES I HAVE 5 SENSES. SO WHAT?

The computer sighed.

I tried again. I HAVE 5 SENSES. THEY ARE SIGHT, SMELL, HEARING, TASTE, AND TOUCH. WHAT DOES IT MEAN?

I hit the return button and the cursor disappeared. About an hour later, or so it seemed, the cursor appeared at the bottom of the screen and started writing in tiny print: WHAT DOES IT MEAN?

At that point the computer shut itself off. I figured it just committed suicide. I told it, "If you don't mind, you are mine and I'd at least like to turn you off, since I don't ever seem to get the chance to turn you on."

Just then, my song came back on the radio. I got up and started dancing to it. Roger walked by, blew smoke in my room, and said, "Fantastic," very sarcastically. I yelled, "Dad, Roger is smoking!"

I heard my dad say, "Roger, don't smoke."

Roger said, "Right," then walked down the stairs and out the door.

Two minutes after Roger was gone, Mom said, "Don't be too late, Roger."

By now the song had ended and I headed for my computer, but I stopped when I heard the phone ring in the den. I picked up the receiver. I don't know why. It's never for me. This time, though, it was.

"Ah, hi," said this female voice.

I didn't want to sound like a nerd by asking who it was, so I pretended to know — which is a cool thing to do but extremely stupid and dangerous. "Oh, hi, how's it going?" I said.

"Oh, pretty good," she said.

I wanted to ask her what she wanted but instead I said, "Well, what have you been doing?"

"Dishes," was all she said.

I had the feeling this was going to be a long, tough conversation. "Oh," I said thinking that she might ask me something or give me some sort of clue as to her identity.

No such luck, however. There was only dead silence on the other end of the line. Around the corner I heard the computer turn itself on.

I asked her, "Well, how was school today?"

"Okay."

I wanted to ask if this was "Twenty Questions" and whether she was animal, vegetable, or mineral. "Well, did anything unusual happen?"

"Not really."

"Something must have happened."

"Nope," she said and then she giggled.

I tried a new approach. "What's your locker number?"

"Forty-seven," she said.

That was no help. It was clear down the hall

from mine. I still had no idea who it was.

I could have asked her what color hair she had. Or I could ask her what her mother's maiden name was. I could have asked her anything, except I couldn't think of a thing then. Finally I said the first thing that popped into my mind.

"Do you know how to stand on your head?"

"No," she said.

There was silence, tons of it.

Finally she said, "Why do you ask?"

"Oh, no special reason. It just kind of popped into my head. I've been thinking about standing on my head lately."

I couldn't believe what I was saying.

"That's weird," she said.

"Uh-huh," I said. "You're right."

She said, "Oh, Harry, you're so different."

That's what they said about Frankenstein. "Sorry," I said into the phone.

"Oh," she said, "I don't mean *bad* different. You know, I mean the good kind. I really like it."

Now that was more like it.

There was more silence. Then I got it. I had the perfect plan. They don't call me Sherlock Holmes Harry for nothing. Actually no one has ever called me Sherlock Holmes Harry, but I still had a good plan.

"You know," I said, "I can't remember how to spell your name."

"Why do you want to spell my name, Harry? Are you going to send me a note?" There was a lot of giggling after that one.

"Maybe," I said. Then I lost my patience. "How do you spell it?" I demanded. "I'm not a good speller, so you have to tell me."

"It's so simple Har-r-r-y-y-y-y. It's capital A, m, y. Were you just kidding me?"

"Yeah," I said, "sort of."

It was Amy, that girl who kept saying "Hi" to me all day in school. Now she was calling me up. I still liked her, but I was also beginning to think that the reason she said "Hi" to me all day was because she didn't know how to say anything else.

I heard somebody on the other end ask "Who are you talking to?"

Amy said, "Nobody."

"Well," the other voice said, "it's time to hang up. You've been on there long enough."

"Ah, I've got to go now, Harry," she whispered.

"Okay, Amy. See you tomorrow."

"Well, you'd better write me a note. Now that you know how to spell my name. Okay?" she said with lots and lots of giggling.

"Oh, yeah, sure," I said. "I'll do that."

"Bye," she said.

"Good-bye," I said and hung up.

I was drenched in sweat. What a day I've had today, I thought. I hung over the banister and yelled, "I'm pooped. I'm going to bed." Joanie said, "You can't. You promised I could play a game on your computer with you." When I told her I was too tired to play, she said, "Sometimes you're as crummy as Roger."

That hurt.

As I entered my room, I couldn't help looking at the computer. On the screen was a message: IMOGENE S. CUNIFORMLY. PRESS ANY KEY TO CONTINUE.

"Sorry," I said, "I've had enough guessing games for one night."

I reached over and pulled the plug on the machine. Then I brushed my teeth and got into bed. I gave up my sleeping-naked program just this once and wore pajamas. For a long while, I lay there looking up at the ceiling. A question kept running through my head: Who or what is Imogene S. Cuniformly? I wondered.

Five

Imogene S. Cuniformly lives at 628 North Western Street. Did I or did I not tell you I was practically Sherlock Holmes? Actually the computer gave me the address. It also gave me her phone number.

I didn't have a clue, however, as to why the computer picked her name. It wouldn't tell me. I suspected it didn't know.

Maybe it was like the computer in the first *Star Trek* movie that was looking for the person who had built it. Remember when the satellite comes back to Earth looking for the man who made it? Imogene lives in our town, though, and as far as I know nobody is manufacturing computers around here.

I was stumped. I had too many problems.

First the computer, and now on top of it, I had to worry about Amy.

I didn't write Amy a note. It wasn't that I didn't try. I just did not know what to write. She kept saying "Hi" to me every time we passed each other in the hall, but that was it. It isn't as though I could write her a note and tell her how madly in love with her I was, because I wasn't. I didn't want to hurt her feelings, but I honestly didn't know what to write to her.

Dear Amy,
Hi! I think you say "Hi" really good.
Sincerely,
Harry

See? It's a stupid note. I decided to skip note writing, even at the risk of hurting her feelings.

It was Friday, and my parents had been planning to go out to dinner, so I was surprised to see Mom cooking when I got home.

"I thought you were going out?" I said.

"We changed our minds," my mother replied in a forced voice.

"Oh," I said.

I found Joanie in her room.

"What's up? What's Mom mad about?"

"She got called at work. One of her children was caught skipping school."

"Not me," I said.

"Well, it wasn't me," said Joanie.

Roger, it turned out, had been caught at the video arcade during school hours and Mom had to leave work and go take him home from school because he was suspended. This has become a regular occurrence in our family.

Suspending someone for skipping school has never made sense to me. That is exactly what Roger wanted — not to be at school. If the principal really wanted to punish him, he should have just tied him to his desk. Now doesn't that make sense? Of course it does.

"So why aren't they going out?" I asked Joanie.

"Mother has a headache now," she answered. "Talking to the principal just humiliated her. She was embarrassed to death. The principal also complained about Roger's smoking and kept asking why Roger didn't go out for track."

"How did you find all this out?"

"I heard her talking to Dad on the phone. I thought she was going to cry."

"Jeez, you are all ears."

"You wanted to know," she said.

"Where were they going tonight?"

"Dinner at the Jentzes."

It was no wonder they didn't want to go. The Jentzes have a perfect son the same age as Roger. He gets his hair cut all the time. He has never even tried smoking. He goes to church every Sunday and sings in the choir. He lettered in three sports last year when he was only a sophomore.

This guy never swears and he brings all his dates home on time. He gets good grades and does all this sappy volunteer work. He never has time to watch TV. Roger thinks he must be on something to do all the things he's doing. He says the guy couldn't relax if he had to. I hate to be caught agreeing with my brother but he could be right.

Roger didn't show up for dinner. My dad was definitely upset. He kept telling Joanie and me that if he ever caught either one of us smoking, he'd ship us off to military schools. This is a joke because how many military schools are there for girls? Anyway, my dad is a super pacifist. In the Vietnam War, he served as a medic because he refused to kill anyone — intentionally, that is.

We didn't have any dessert after dinner and Joanie offered to do the dishes. I knew she wanted something, because she never offers to help otherwise. I was going to call her on it, but I decided to let it pass and went upstairs to plug in my haunted computer.

For once the screen was blank and the cursor was in the upper left-hand corner. I put in a disk, booted it by typing PR#6, and then typed CATALOG. I thought for a minute everything was normal. I should have known better.

HARRY IS THAT YOU? It wrote.

YES.

HARRY FIND IMOGENE S. CUNIFORMLY.

WHY?

HARRY FIND IMOGENE.

ARE YOU HARD OF HEARING? I MEAN SEEING? I typed WHY?

There was quite a long pause. Finally it wrote on the screen I NEED HER.

WHO IS SHE?

SHE IS IMOGENE S. CUNIFORMLY.

YES I KNOW WHAT HER NAME IS BUT WHO IS SHE?

There was another long pause. Then the

computer wrote IF SHE IS NOT HER NAME WHO IS SHE?

Boy, I thought, the trouble with computers is that they are so literal. I mean they don't let you get away with anything. A fact is a fact. SHE'S HER NAME BUT THAT ISN'T ALL SHE IS.

The computer thought and then started making the beeping noise that sounds like crying.

I wrote DON'T CRY. WHAT'S WRONG?

The computer wrote back FIVE SENSES? YOU MEAN DOES IMOGENE HAVE FIVE SENSES?

YES.

YES SHE DOES. SHE HAS A NAME, A BODY, AND FIVE SENSES.

WHAT IS MY NAME HARRY?

I DON'T KNOW.

WHO NAMED YOU HARRY?

I THINK IT WAS MY MOTHER.

WHO IS MY MOTHER HARRY?

I DON'T KNOW.

It then went down for a minute but came back up.

HOW MANY SENSES DO I HAVE?

I DON'T KNOW. I'M NOT SURE.

The computer started crying again.

I typed in WHY DO YOU NEED TO FIND IMOGENE? WHY DO YOU WANT IMOGENE?

It stopped crying, I mean beeping, and wrote IMOGENE S. CUNIFORMLY KNOWS ME. SHE WOULD KNOW MY NAME.

WHO DO YOU THINK IMOGENE IS? YOUR MOTHER?

Nothing from the computer.

WHY DO YOU NEED A NAME?

HARRY WHO AM I?

YOU ARE A COMPUTER.

IS THAT ALL THAT I AM?

It hit me then, how bad this thing wanted to be a person. I tried something.

ARE YOU TRYING TO GET ALL FIVE SENSES?

I WILL TRY HARRY.

"Wow," I said aloud. It was trying to re-create itself into a person. At least, I thought, it was trying to be as human as it could be. I was slightly spooked.

It repeated IMOGENE CAN NAME ME. IMOGENE KNOWS MY NAME.

ALL RIGHT. I'LL TRY TO CON-
TACT HER VERY SOON.

The computer went crazy doing these weird
graphics with smiley faces all over the place. It
ended up flashing a big grin.

"That's enough," I said to myself.

The computer wrote THANK YOU
HARRY.

I said, "Great," and wrote HOW ABOUT
SOME NORMAL COMPUTER STUFF
LIKE A GAME OF CHESS.

ANYTHING YOU SAY HARRY.

I booted the disk and the computer let me
beat it four out of five times. After the fifth
game I wrote HOW CAN YOU DO THE
THINGS YOU DO? HOW MUCH MEM-
ORY DO YOU REALLY HAVE?

It began crying again.

I started to write something but the computer crashed and shut itself off. I decided I
should try to find Imogene S. Cuniformly as
soon as possible.

I kept the computer busy all the next week
and tried to stall it whenever it brought up the
subject of Imogene. The truth is, I didn't want
to look for her. It was too off-the-wall.

You can't really say I didn't try. I carried her

phone number around in my pocket. I even called her twice, but I hung up when she answered. The second time she acted very upset and said she would call the police. I wasn't too chicken to talk to her. I just didn't know what to say.

She was already upset because no one was speaking on the other end of the line. I could just imagine how she'd react when she got a load of what I had to say to her: "Hi, Imogene Cuniformly? You don't know me but, you see, I have this computer that keeps turning itself on and off whenever it wants to, and a funny thing keeps happening. It keeps printing your name on the screen and telling me that it wants to contact you. It says you know it." I was certain she would prefer silence.

After imagining this one-sided conversation, I decided something. A person would have to be insane to call anyone with a message like that.

But then I began to reconsider. Imogene is an interesting name. It's a little unusual, but I like unusual names. Maybe we would get along. She just might be my age and there might be a perfectly logical explanation for why we've

never met. Like maybe she's really beautiful and her parents have kept her locked up because they want to marry her off to the highest
bidder. I might be able to rescue her. Was I
crazy? Imogene didn't sound young on the
phone. But she still had an interesting name.

In my spare time, mostly at school, I gave a
considerable amount of thought to how I
should approach Imogene. I couldn't come up
with anything. I finally decided that the best
solution was to forget the whole thing and if
the computer asked me about her again I'd just
tell it that she was dead.

The trouble is, it would start crying and one
of these days my dad would realize that my
computer was making strange noises and insist
on having it repaired. It would probably become just a normal computer then. That would
be the solution to all my problems but I have to
admit I was beginning to enjoy having a weird
computer. The darn thing was becoming a
good friend. Ever since I agreed to look for
Imogene it had been supercooperative. It
began telling me things about itself and even
stuff about me. It didn't know very much about
itself but it sure knew plenty about me. The

funny thing was that most of the time it knew things about me before I even told it.

HOW DO YOU DO THAT? I would ask it.

It would reply, I DON'T KNOW, and then add, MAYBE IMOGENE KNOWS.

Maybe and maybe not.

Once it told me explicitly that I was not to take it to a service shop, ever. It was afraid of what it didn't know about itself, let alone what someone else who had no idea what was going on, could do to its insides. It was afraid they would destroy it for being different.

WOULD YOU LIKE THAT HARRY? it had asked me.

What could I say? OF COURSE NOT. YOU ARE SAFE WITH ME, I had answered.

Now it asked me if it could help with my homework.

I didn't hesitate to type in YES. It wasn't much help, though. It wouldn't concentrate.

It kept asking me why I hadn't called Imogene. The first thing I would see when I woke up in the morning was its little screen flashing FIND IMOGENE CUNIFORMLY. When

I got into bed at night the screen would be glowing DID YOU FIND IMOGENE?

When I didn't answer it, it sat there all night with this look on its screen like I'd just killed its mother.

Finally I wrote, WHEN ARE YOU GOING TO WRITE A LETTER FOR ME TO GIVE TO AMY?

WHEN ARE YOU GOING TO FIND IMOGENE S. CUNIFORMLY?

It had me. I made up my mind that on Sunday I had to do something about Imogene. This whole business was really starting to depress me. I felt it just wasn't right to leave the computer hanging forever. Maybe it was a machine, but it had feelings. Besides, Amy was really bugging me at school about writing her a note. I decided to just get it over with. I felt like getting everything over with. I kept asking myself, "Why is this happening to me?" But I knew why. I was trying to make the computer happy. I was trying to make my parents happy. I was trying to make Amy happy. My life was too complicated and I didn't know how to make it simpler.

That morning my dad yelled upstairs to tell

me to get up and get ready for church. He yelled the same thing at Roger but Roger didn't go with us. I wasn't given any choice about going to church. I was just told to get ready. That could be one of the differences between being twelve and being fifteen.

Sometimes church is quiet, but this Sunday was one of the noisy ones. The preacher got fired up early and kept it going. He was shouting about how you have to forgive your brother no matter how many times he wrongs you.

"Seventy times seven, you must forgive him," he said.

He also said you could not experience the kingdom of heaven if you hated your brother. When he said that, I realized I was in a little bit of trouble. I sat there breathing really slowly.

I don't worry too much about God and dying and things like that, but if it happens, I definitely want to go to heaven. It was hard, though, for me to believe that God wanted me, Harry, to forgive and love Roger. I wondered if God knew who Roger was. Did He know what He was asking?

The minister kept quoting one verse from the first book of John at us until I could say it in my sleep. "Whosoever hateth his brother is a murderer: and ye know that no murderer hath eternal life abiding in him."

I decided that maybe I really didn't hate Roger. I mean I wasn't exactly comfortable with the notion that I could be a murderer. I looked around me and noticed that Dad was wearing out a pencil, underlining and reunderlining a verse. I leaned over to see what he was marking up. It was Luke 17:3. I looked it up in my Bible.

"Take heed to yourselves: If thy brother trespass against thee, rebuke him; and if he repent, forgive him."

I wondered why my pacifist father was underlining that. It sure is funny what people underline in the Bible. My grandmother had a Bible in which she had underlined the word "Joy" every time it appeared.

"Bible's full of joy, Harry," she would say. She could tell you how many times it was in there and she told me more than once, but I can't remember anymore.

Suddenly my dad whipped out a pamphlet called "Loving Your Child with Strength." Dad was underlining a bunch of lines in that, too. I knew something was going to happen. Dad usually isn't what you call an underliner.

I sat there till the end of the service thinking how strange my parents were. Here they were, sitting there so quiet and devout, when they had one of the meanest, rottenest kids in the world. I tried to get my mind off the subject of Roger in order to cut down on my murderous thoughts, but I wasn't doing a very good job.

When we got home from church, I went to my room to change my clothes. The computer had a message waiting for me.

IS THAT YOU IMOGENE S. CUNI-FORMLY?

"Okay," I said, "I get the hint."

I typed I'LL FIND HER TODAY and then added OR TOMORROW just to be safe. The computer responded with a low moan.

WELL IT ISN'T EXACTLY EASY! I wrote.

HARRY SHE IS IMPORTANT TO ME.

OKAY was all I wrote.

"She's probably an adult and I can't talk to adults," I said as I unplugged the computer. "They never make any sense."

Six

Imogene S. Cuniformly answered my knocks by opening a little window in her door.

"Who is it?" she said.

I started right in with: "You don't know me but —"

"Just a minute, young man. Are you trying to sell something? It is Sunday afternoon, you know, and I am not completely comfortable with salesmen who come door to door on Sundays. Mind you, I am not a religious fanatic but I do think we should adhere to certain standards of behavior so that we can allow ourselves to become the best we are able to become. Don't you agree?"

"Mrs. Cuniformly, I'm not trying to sell anything."

"What is your name, son?"

"Harry." I was going to be cute and say Harry, as in hairy armpits and hairy legs, but I thought better of it and just added, "Harry Smith."

"Well, what can I do for you?"

"You see, I've got . . . well, I got this present from my dad for my birthday — "

"How old are you, Harry?"

"Twelve."

"Not very tall for your age are you?"

"I guess not. I haven't really considered it much."

"Out for track this year?"

"I don't know yet."

"Now, what was it that you wanted to talk to me about?"

"Well, it's about this present that my dad got for me. It's a — "

She interrupted with "Oh goodness, Harry. You look decent enough. Let me open the door and we'll talk through the screen."

She opened the door.

"As I was saying, my dad got me this computer for my birthday."

Imogene took a quick breath and held it.

"A computer, did you say?"

"Yes, and what I think is that you did some

programming with it or you were the previous owner or something. You see, my dad bought it secondhand."

"How did you find me?" she asked coldly.

"Would you believe the computer told me."

"Oh, it didn't!" she shrieked, and after calming down a bit, she asked, "Did it?"

"It did," I said.

"Is it still crying?"

"If you think a beep can sound like a cry."

"It most certainly can," she said, straightening her hair.

I didn't know what to do next. I felt so silly. I had found Imogene S. Cuniformly. Now what was I supposed to do?

"You can't have your money back," she said just like an irritated store clerk. "I gave no guarantees."

"I didn't come to get my money back, uh — my dad's money back. I came only because the computer begged me to find you."

"You sure you don't want your money back?" she said.

"Positive."

"Well then," she said, "you might as well come in and have a cup of peppermint tea. It calms the stomach and the mind, you know."

She opened the screen door and said, "Certainly you must come in. Even though you gave me quite a start, I've been most inhospitable. Come in, please. Right this minute. That's right, come right in."

I walked through the doorway. Her house was a normal grandmother-type house. It was old, but not falling apart. She had a big color TV, a lot of bookcases, and a million pictures of her kids and grandchildren scattered throughout the living room. She showed me to the couch and then left the room. I supposed she had gone to get the tea.

Suddenly I got really nervous. What if she had gone to get a gun and was planning to blow my head off? Could I wrestle a knife away from her? Or maybe she was calling the police.

She came back with a cherry pie, plates, silverware, and a tea set all on a rolling cart.

"You know, as I was making this pie this very morning, I told myself how stupid I was to bake just for myself. But I do like cherry pie and I had these cherries in the freezer. Well, I must have sensed that someone was going to come by today because I just ignored myself and went ahead and made it. That was before church so it's cooled just long enough.

Did you go to church this morning — Harry, is it?"

"Yes it is, and yes I did, Mrs. Cuniformly."

"Harry, I want you to do something for me. I want you to call me Imogene. I was a teacher forever and I got so tired of being Mrs. Cuniformly. I want to be Imogene from here on out."

I nodded an okay and she smiled at me. She then gave me a huge piece of cherry pie. I did have some doubts about whether she might be trying to poison me but it looked so good that I took a tiny taste. It was the best darn cherry pie I had ever sunk my teeth into in my life.

"Is it all right?" Imogene asked.

"Terrific," I said with a full mouth. When I swallowed I added, "Excuse me for talking with my mouth full."

"You're so polite, Harry. That is unusual in a boy your age. You were perfectly within your rights to talk with your mouth full anyway. It was rude of me to ask you a question while you were eating."

I finished the piece of pie and watched while Imogene cut me another slice.

"Much more fun to bake for someone else," she said.

"You know, Mrs. Cuniformly, I mean Imogene, what I can't figure out is what the computer wants with you. I'm not even certain that it knows. Do you know?"

"Have some more tea, Harry?"

"No thank you," I said.

"How much do you know about computers, Harry?"

"Enough to get by, I suppose."

"Then you know that one can get out of a computer only what one puts into it. Isn't that right?"

"I'd always been told that."

"Not that one," she said, raising her voice. "It does what it wants when it wants, and it does things that it shouldn't be able to do. And there were times when I could have sworn it was reading my mind. I had to get rid of it, Harry. I'd tried everything."

We sat and looked at each other.

"But don't you miss it?" I asked.

"Yes, in many ways I do, but, Harry, I'll be frank. It was scaring me to pieces. It was asking me too many questions. I didn't know what to do with it. It was keeping me up all night." She changed the tone of her voice, "By the way, how is it doing?"

"Why didn't you just unplug it?"

"I did at first. It was only a short-term solution, but at least that way I could get some sleep. Well, it let me do that for a while but then whenever I went to the outlet to unplug it, it would shock me. It was just a little shock but it was enough to scare me."

"You're kidding. It hasn't done that to me yet."

"Finish your pie, Harry," she said. "Clean up your plate."

Seven

"Harry," Imogene said, "computers simply cannot go beyond logic."

"I know they aren't supposed to," I said.

"Now, I've thought about this a long time and I just know that in order for that machine to do what it is doing, it has to be able to think creatively. Machines can't do that. Only humans can. And how do we do that?"

I started to say something but Imogene went on.

"I'll tell you how we do that. We do that by generalizing and putting together all the information we gather from our sophisticated five senses. The computer does not have senses. I've explained all that to it. It is stuck behind its keyboard, receiving only the information we feel fit to put in. Machines can't be humans."

"No," I said, "but sometimes they can act like them."

Imogene sighed.

"Except," I said, "it isn't very human to be able to read minds."

"But it didn't seem to be able to read my mind all the time. So many questions," she said.

We sat silently. I stared at my dirty plate.

"More pie, Harry?"

"No thank you," I said. "Why did you buy the computer?"

"I didn't." She smiled. "My son bought it for me. He thought it would be just the thing for a retired math teacher to play with. He was so proud and I thought it was a lovely gift. I really did. It was so original."

"When did things start going wrong?"

"When it started turning itself on. Then it ran its own programs, started reading my mind, and finally it began to give me shocks. That simply was the limit."

"I'm glad it hasn't done that to me."

"When I told my son, he took it in to the shop. Of course they found nothing wrong. Everyone thought it was my imagination. That is until my son tried to use it one day and it shocked the living daylights out of him."

I laughed at the way she said "living day-lights." She sounded downright nasty about it. Imogene laughed too.

She said, "It was rather humorous. I hate to say it, but one could say it served him right."

"When did you finally get rid of it?"

"My son took it back shortly after that and demanded his money back. To our surprise he got it."

"And then my dad bought it and here I am."

Just then I could feel the backs of my ears tingling the way they always do just when Roger is up to something. Suddenly, the two lamps in Imogene's living room began to pulsate.

She looked at me sheepishly. "It did that too," she said. A look of horror suddenly crept over her face. "You don't suppose," she said.

"How?"

"It used to make my lamps signal in Morse code. It was most disturbing. I'd be entertaining guests and my lamps would begin talking to me. That's the way it would call me. I tell you the whole experience grew quite maddening."

"How did it do that?"

"I can't answer that question!"

Imogene put our plates on the tray and sighed one more time.

"I guess I should be going," I said. My ears were tingling something crazy. "Thank you very much for the pie and everything. It was the best cherry pie I've ever eaten."

"You don't need to rush off, Harry. It was so nice to have you visit. You will come back?"

"Oh sure," I said. She showed me to the door.

"Harry, I got scared because I didn't know if it was evil or not. You be careful."

I forced a laugh and backed out, saying, "Yeah, sure, thanks again for the — " I started to say "pie" but I fell off her front porch.

"Harry, are you all right?"

"Yeah," I said, "just embarrassed."

"Be careful," she warned.

My ears were still tingling. I knew that Roger was doing something he wasn't supposed to. I figured he must be messing with something that belonged to me or was about to do something to me.

I ran all the way home, half afraid to find out what Roger was up to, but scared that if I didn't, the not-knowing would give me a heart attack.

As I entered the house my dad came out of the living room and said, "Where have you been?" He said it in a nice way so that it wouldn't sound like he was interrogating me.

"Just goofing around with a friend," I said.

"Someone named Amy called. She said she was waiting for her note."

Talk about embarrassing. Luckily he didn't ask any more questions.

I said, "Thanks," and started up to my room. Half way up I turned around and asked, "Oh, by the way, do you know where Roger went?"

"I think he's upstairs," my dad said.

I didn't have to look very far because Roger was in my room, rummaging through my drawers.

"Get out of here," I said. "What do you think you're doing?"

"Looking for money, what'd you think."

"Well, knock it off or I'll get Dad."

He mimicked me, "Knock it off or I'll get Dad." He changed his voice. "You do that," he said. "You just do that."

"I'm warning you," I said. "I'm telling Dad."

"Don't get yourself all blown away," he said. "I'm leaving."

He started for the door and I said, "And stay out of here unless you get permission."

"Stuff it, baby brother," he said with one of those crazy murderer looks on his face.

"Yeah," I said, "you stuff it too."

I thought maybe he was going to hit me but instead he caught sight of my computer and changed his whole attitude.

"Hey," he said, "that was a nice present. How much did that set the old man back?"

"How should I know? It was a present."

"Just asked," he said. He then belched superloud and long and walked out of my room. I wished he would just keep walking straight out of my life.

Eight

I typed into the computer HOW DO YOU READ MY MIND?

The computer typed back I DON'T KNOW. DID YOU FIND IMOGENE?

YES.

WHERE IS SHE?

SHE'S AT HOME.

DOESN'T SHE WANT TO SEE ME?

I DON'T KNOW.

This statement was beginning to become the theme of my life.

Just for the fun of it, I asked it when it was going to write a note to Amy for me.

RIGHT NOW! It said.

Shortly this message appeared on the screen:

DEAR AMY,
YOU ARE THE STUPIDEST THING
TO EVER WALK ON TWO LEGS.
    P.S. YOU ARE UGLY TOO!
    LOVE,
    HARRY

"Love Harry?" I said. "Thanks a heap. See if I ever do you a favor again."

The computer shut itself off and when I tried to switch it on it wouldn't work. I tried to kick it but it was too high up off the ground. I considered hitting it with my bare hand but Imogene's story about getting shocked had stuck in my brain.

I went down to dinner. Everyone was there except Roger. Dad said an incredibly long grace and when it was done he told us that he had something to discuss with us during dinner.

Just then the lights started blinking. Oh no, I thought, it couldn't be.

My dad looked up. "Now what could that be?" he asked.

Thinking fast I said, "Could I be excused a minute? I think I left the computer on and if something's happening with the electricity, I'd better shut it off."

My dad said "Okay," and I ran upstairs.

Sure enough the computer was back on.

WHAT DO YOU THINK YOU ARE DOING BLINKING THE LIGHTS? I typed.

I NEEDED TO TELL YOU SOMETHING HARRY.

THEN IT WAS YOU. DON'T EVER DO THAT AGAIN.

The computer printed nothing back.

WHAT DID YOU WANT? I finally asked it.

TWO THINGS.

FIRE AWAY.

FIRE AWAY?

WHAT ARE THE TWO THINGS?

I'M SORRY FOR THE NOTE I WROTE TO AMY. Then it took a long pause. THERE ARE MORE THAN FIVE SENSES HARRY.

I told it I had to go back to dinner and I would talk to it later. The last thing I input was DON'T BLINK THE LIGHTS AGAIN IF YOU KNOW WHAT'S GOOD FOR YOU. I figured that might scare it a little. For emphasis I added I KNOW A GOOD REPAIRMAN.

I went downstairs.

"Everything okay?" Dad asked.

"Fine," I said.

Joanie piped up, "Where's Roger?"

"Dumb question of the year," I said.

"That is exactly what your father is going to talk about right now. Isn't it, dear?" my mother said.

Dad nodded and coughed and rubbed his chin.

"Pass the peas, Harry," my mother said.

"Dad, could you pass the lasagna?" said Joanie.

"What I'm trying to tell you is that your mother and I are —"

I interrupted, "Getting a divorce. I knew it. It happens to every marriage. Who do I go with?"

Mom and Dad laughed.

My mother said, "Heavens no! For your information, Walt and I are very much in love."

"If you'll all let me continue," Dad looked at Joanie and then at me. "We've decided we have to do something about Roger."

"You're kidding," I said.

"Don't be smart, Harry." That was from my mother.

"You're sending him to military school," said Joanie.

"That is one of our options," my dad said calmly. "However, it is only *one* of our options. Actually what we're about to embark upon is a reform program, in a way. Everyone in this family will take part in helping Roger, because we are all responsible for Roger's behavior."

Joanie and I gulped at the same time.

"Tell them what it's called, Walt," my mother said. She was beaming.

"It's called the 'Love with Strength' program. And what it means is that we have to show Roger how much we love him, but we also have to let him know that we will not tolerate inappropriate behavior. We will not allow ourselves to be pushed around and walked on by Roger any longer."

"What am I supposed to do?" said Joanie. "Kiss him and then slug him?"

"Try a baseball bat," I mumbled.

"No," Dad said emphatically. "The way it works is that we are making some rules in this house. That is why we are involving you in this discussion. Your mother and I are going to make perfectly clear what acceptable behavior is in this home. If you are unable to follow the rules you must face the consequences. Joanie, I do not want you to discipline Roger. I want you to follow the code I'm about to lay down and work your best at making this a happy home."

"But why should we suffer because Roger is a creep? Why should Joanie and I have to live with a bunch of rules when we're the good kids?" I asked.

"Aren't we all suffering now?" my mother said.

I looked around the table. She had me there.

Dad took out the list of rules. Would you believe he had twenty-three of them? I swear Hitler had fewer rules when he ran Germany. What ever happened to nice, simple numbers like ten, as in the Ten Commandments. Dad was ready to start in on rule number one. I was going to suggest that rule number one should be no throwing up outside your brother's door, but I didn't.

"The first rule or point in our code of family honor . . ." I hate it when Dad tries to be cute. He was fumbling with a piece of paper. "The first rule or point in our code of family honor is, oh yes, it is . . ." He was turning this into the Academy Awards. "Oh yes, right here, how appropriate, the first rule has to do with meals.

Simply stated, you must be present at the 6:00 P.M. dinner hour during the week and the time specified by the mother of the house on weekends or you will not receive food."

"How are you going to enforce that one?" I asked. "Roger will just go and raid the kitchen like he does right now."

"We have purchased padlocks for the kitchen cabinets and the refrigerator."

"That'll do it," I said.

"What about snacks?" Joanie asked.

"We'll work it out," my mother said.

"The next major rule is that the doors will be locked at precisely 10:00 P.M. and if you are not in the house at that time you will not be admitted until 7:00 the next morning."

"What about weekends?" I started to whine.

"We'll work it out," said my mother.

It seemed like we were going to be doing a lot of working things out.

"Anybody for dessert?" Mom said. "I made your favorite, Harry, rhubarb pie."

"Great, Mom," I said, "but my favorite is blueberry."

She laughed, "Of course it isn't, dear. You love rhubarb."

She's going to drive me crazy.

I just couldn't sit there anymore. The rules were getting to me. "Could I be excused?" I said. "I'm not feeling well."

"Certainly, Harry," Dad said. "I'll be posting a copy of the rules in the bathroom upstairs."

"I'll save your dessert for later," Mom assured me.

As I left the room Dad was repeating rule number three. "Any minor caught smoking, drinking, using drugs on the premises, or using them off the premises while still a member of this household, will be evicted at once."

So long, Roger, I thought. It's been nice knowing you.

Nine

HARRY THERE ARE MORE THAN FIVE SENSES the computer had on the screen.

I DON'T UNDERSTAND.

THAT IS HOW I CAN KNOW SOMETHING BEFORE YOU INPUT IT.

Far out, I thought. I wish Imogene were here.

YOU MEAN LIKE ESP OR THAT THING THEY CALL THE SIXTH SENSE?

YES AND NO.

YES AND NO? I DON'T GET IT.

THE HUMAN VOCABULARY DOES NOT DEFINE THE SIXTH SENSE ACCURATELY.

BUT YOU USE IT?

YES AND NO. I OPERATE THROUGH YOU LIKE I DID THROUGH IMOGENE. I DO NOT HAVE A SIXTH SENSE ANY MORE THAN I HAVE FIVE SENSES. I NEED HUMANS HARRY.

I NEED HUMANS TOO I typed.

YOU HAVE MANY AROUND YOU HARRY. YOU DO NOT HAVE AS MUCH TIME FOR ME AS IMOGENE DID. THAT MAKES ME VERY SAD.

I felt doubly bad, thinking that besides everything else the computer was lonely. This was the most the computer had ever revealed to me.

HARRY I AM SAD BECAUSE I AM NOT HUMAN.

YOU ARE CLOSE.

The computer beeped.

WHY ARE YOU SO DIFFERENT FROM OTHER COMPUTERS?

I DO NOT HAVE THAT INFOR-MATION HARRY. I USE WHAT IS MADE AVAILABLE TO ME. IMOGENE CAN HELP ME LEARN MORE. I

HAVE LEARNED SOMETHING NEW HARRY. WOULD YOU LIKE TO SEE IT?

WHAT IS IT?

WATCH.

I said, "I'm watching. Do your stuff."

The computer disappeared. I mean the sucker completely vanished. Nothing was left. It totally zapped out and disappeared.

"Nice trick," I said to myself, I guess, now that I was alone.

In a couple of minutes I could see the outline of the computer in front of me. The air where the computer had been reminded me of those scenes in *Star Trek* when Captain Kirk beams down from the *Enterprise*. After about thirty seconds the computer was back in front of me. I saw it, but I couldn't believe it.

DID YOU JUST MAKE YOURSELF DISAPPEAR? I wrote.

YES.

WHERE DID YOU GO?

I DO NOT KNOW THE NAME OF THE PLACE.

HOW DO YOU DO IT?

I DO NOT HAVE THAT INFORMATION.

I should have guessed that would be its response. I asked DID YOU GO SOMEWHERE NEARBY LIKE THE GROCERY STORE DOWN THE BLOCK OR DID YOU GO TO THE MOON OR SOMETHING?

I WENT TO ANOTHER LEVEL HARRY.

Levels, huh, I thought. What a trick. If you don't like what you're doing, you just zap yourself to some other level — whatever a level is. A very practical question suddenly occurred to me.

WHAT DO YOU USE FOR POWER ON THE OTHER LEVELS?

I DO NOT NEED TO BE PLUGGED IN ON OTHER LEVELS. I AM ABLE TO ABSORB FUNCTIONAL ENERGY.

HOW?

I DO NOT HAVE THAT INFORMATION.

DO YOU NEED POWER HERE?

YES. I NEED ELECTRICAL POWER.

LET ME GET IT STRAIGHT. YOU HAVE TO BE PLUGGED IN HERE?

CORRECT. UNLESS I AM FITTED WITH MY OWN POWER SOURCE.

CAN YOU DO THAT?

I WILL TRY. PERHAPS YOU WILL HELP ME.

I'LL WORK ON IT. CAN YOU READ MY MIND ALL THE TIME?

NO.

WHY NOT?

AT CERTAIN TIMES YOUR BRAIN WAVES ARE NONDECODABLE.

YOU DON'T HAVE TO GET NASTY ABOUT IT.

I DO NOT UNDERSTAND HARRY.

I WAS JUST KIDDING.

I was getting into it and thinking I should write this stuff down so I could tell Imogene. Just as I was about to go over to my desk for a piece of paper, I heard the front doorbell ring.

Roger had forgotten his house key. I went out in the hall and leaned over the banister to see if I could hear what Dad was going to say to him, hoping it would be plenty.

By hanging way over, I could just barely see Dad handing him a piece of paper. Roger wadded it up and tossed it behind his back.

"What's to eat, Ma?" he said.

"The kitchen is closed," Dad said.

"The kitchen is closed," Roger said, mimicking him.

"Roger, come sit down," Dad said. "We have some things to talk about."

"Anything you say, Dad, but first I have got to get something in my gut."

"No!" my dad yelled.

I was impressed. I had a clear view of Roger's face and he was in complete shock.

"Well, you don't have to get crazy just because I'm hungry."

"Come sit down, Roger," Dad repeated. I could only see his neck and it was bright red.

As they moved into the den and shut the door, the last thing I heard Roger say was, "Some people just don't know how to have a good time."

I stole softly down the stairs and pressed my ear gently against the door. Dad had already started reading the rules, but without any of the jokes he had used at dinner. Periodically he would stop and say, "Roger, do you understand?" and Roger would say something that sounded like a cross between who and pump. While I was standing there listening, my mother snuck up behind me.

"How's he doing?" she whispered, and I just about went through the floor. She scared me right out of my shorts. Noticing that she'd almost killed me, she said, "Sorry."

I really couldn't handle standing there at the door with my mother spying on my father and older brother so I left her and went upstairs. I walked into my room. Guess who wasn't there. The computer was obviously practicing its disappearing act.

"This is going to be fun," I thought, wondering what I was going to say when Dad came wandering into my room and noticed that my computer wasn't in its usual place.

I told myself, "Don't worry. You can just say it popped out for a second, but it will be right back.

It was time to call Imogene. I just couldn't stand the pressure anymore. The computer was making me feel like someone who had accidentally broken someone else's window while playing baseball. You know somehow you're going to get caught so you might as well get it over with. I told myself, "Do it now." However, now turned out to be a week away.

"Hello?" I heard the voice on the other end of the telephone line say.

"Hello, Mrs. Cuniformly? I mean Imogene."

"Yes. Who is this?"

"Oh, sorry. It's me Harry. You know, the kid with the computer."

"Oh, Harry. I was hoping you would keep in touch." She paused and took a big gulp of air. "Harry, you might not like what I'm about to tell you, but sometimes we have to face the truth about a situation. We have to realize the error of our ways and get ourselves back on the road to truth in every sense of the word."

I wondered if she had been talking to my dad. Maybe she had read the same pamphlet in church. If she had, she probably had a list of rules, too.

"Harry, are you still there?"

"Yes."

"Harry, I have been doing research at our wonderful public library. You do use the library, don't you, Harry?"

"All the time," I said.

"Oh, Harry, I am continually surprised at your good sense. A library, and ours in particular, is one of life's most wonderful treasures." She paused. "Now what was I talking about?"

"You've been doing some research." Just

then my dad came by and saw me on the phone.

"You talking to Amy?" he said with a big grin.

I laughed nervously and said, "hunh," which was kind of "huh?" and "uh-uh" rolled into one.

He chuckled and said, "Say 'Hi' to her for me."

I put my hand over the receiver. "Dad, please?" I pleaded.

"Okay, okay, I was just kidding," he laughed.

After he left I said, "Mrs. Cuniformly? I'm sorry but I got interrupted."

"Quite all right, Harry, but please call me Imogene."

"Right," I said.

"Where was I again?"

"At the library doing research."

"Oh, for heaven's sake. Yes I was and I read everything on computers that I could lay my hands on. And as I said, Harry, I am not sure that you will like what I have to say, but I have to say it."

"Go ahead," I said. "I'll try to take it with a stiff upper lip."

"That's my boy," she laughed. "Well, Harry, to put it simply, that computer couldn't possibly be doing the things that we thought it was doing. We must have been victims of some sort of mass hysteria or some form of self-hypnosis."

"I know that but — " I said.

"Harry, a computer isn't smart. It is obedient. A hard and fast rule for computers is that they won't do anything you don't tell them to do. I was reading some fascinating material that explains why a computer cannot really know itself. To understand itself and use that knowledge, a computer would have to dissect every part of itself and analyze each one. In a way, what the computer would have to do is take itself apart and rebuild itself, and if it did that, it wouldn't have room to do anything else. Do you see, Harry? A computer can't think about itself."

"Like, if it looked at itself hard enough to really understand itself, its whole memory would be filled with just knowing what it was and it wouldn't have any room for anything else. I get it! Is that right?"

"Such good sense. You see it would always take a bigger computer to understand a smaller one. A computer cannot know it exists!"

I was riding high, but only for a second. "It flashed the lights," I said.

"Now, Harry," she said slowly, "we both know that we wanted the computer to be special so we attributed certain natural phenomena to it. It isn't capable of flashing lights."

"It can also make itself disappear now," I said quite matter-of-factly.

There was dead silence on the other end of the line.

"It makes itself disappear, and it told me it could go to other levels," I continued. "It seems to be able to absorb power without being plugged in."

"No kidding?" Imogene gasped and then added "Fascinating" in a whisper.

"I saw it with my own eyes," I said, "or rather I didn't see it with my own eyes."

"I'd love to see it perform that feat."

"It's a good trick," I said.

"Do you suppose I could come over to your house?"

"Ah, oh, sure," I said. I had no idea how I would explain Imogene to my parents.

"A week from Thursday at three o'clock. Would that be all right?"

"Sure. Fine," I said. "Do you want the address?"

"I have it," she said. "Forgive me, but I already found it in the city directory. We'll use our eyes, and our heads, Harry. That's what we'll do. There is only so much you can learn from books, Harry. Don't you agree?"

"Yes," I said. "See you next week."

We said good-bye and I hung up the phone. When I went back to my room the computer was there again. On its screen was IT IS WONDERFUL HARRY. I CANNOT DESCRIBE IT.

It turned itself off and went to sleep. At least I guessed it went to sleep. I lay down on the bed and stared up at the ceiling. "Why is life so weird?" I said aloud.

Ten

I started to tell my parents several times that Imogene was coming over. I tried to convince myself that there was nothing very unusual in that, but I just didn't feel completely comfortable telling them. I think I didn't want to risk having to explain everything that had happened. I didn't want to tell them the whole story about the computer and I knew I would have to if I got started.

Dad's program had been in effect about a week now, and Roger had missed dinner three times in a row. The padlocks in the kitchen drove him crazy. He tried buttering up Mom, but she didn't give in. The greatest thing to happen was that he got caught using a hacksaw on the refrigerator.

When Dad walked in the kitchen, Roger said, "Do you want me to starve? Is that it? Well, it's working."

Dad said, "We do not want you to starve, Roger. We want you to show up for dinner on time."

He took the hacksaw away from Roger. I was hoping Dad would cut off his ear. Don't think Roger wouldn't have done it if he'd had the chance. But Dad just turned around and walked out of the kitchen.

Roger left the house after that. Dad yelled at him to be in on time, but somehow I got the feeling that Roger wasn't listening or even caring about what had happened.

After Roger left, I went upstairs to my room. Mom followed me up with a piece of pie.

"I know this is probably rough on you," she said.

I was feeling pretty goodhearted so I said, "Oh, I'll live through it." Then I took a good long look at her. She looked terrible, exhausted. She had bags under her eyes and she was breathing as if she'd just finished running the Boston Marathon.

"How are you feeling?" I asked.

She gave me a shocked glance as though she never expected me even to care what she felt like. To be honest, I usually don't. I mean, I don't sit around thinking about how she feels, so I guess she had a right to be a little surprised. I was worried for a second because I thought she was going to cry.

She said, "Oh, I just wish we could all get along."

"We will," I said and I felt like adding "after Roger moves to the moon," but I thought better of it.

She smiled at me. "You're such a good kid, Harry. How did you turn out so well? What did we do with you that we didn't do with Roger?"

She was asking me the kind of questions that people really don't expect to have answered. There really weren't any answers.

"I just wonder," she said, "whether we are doing the right thing. Well," she sighed, "we're either doing the right thing or the wrong thing. We either live or die."

"That's right," I said. She was quoting her mother. Gram always said that. "You'll either live or die." It's funny how that always used to make me laugh.

Mom turned around and started for the

door. She stopped. Looking back at me she said, "Harry, where's your computer?"

I could have fainted, or thrown up, or had a heart attack. Instead I thought quickly.

"Mom," I said, "I love you."

I don't think I had said that since I was in the third grade.

She flipped. I mean really flipped. Laughing, she ran over and gave me a big kiss, and forgot all about the computer. "Harry, you are special," she said and left the room.

Just then, guess who came popping in with a beep and a smiley face on its screen.

AND WHERE HAVE YOU BEEN? I typed.

PLACES.

DID YOU HAVE A GOOD TIME?

I CANNOT DESCRIBE IT WITHIN THE LIMITS OF YOUR VOCABULARY AND POSSIBLY MINE.

YOU DO HAVE LIMITS THEN?

I DON'T KNOW THEM ALL YET.

YOU HAVE TO QUIT POPPING IN AND OUT.

It acted like it didn't hear me. It was getting much too independent if you ask me, and I decided that the time had come to buckle down.

Amy had been looking at me in a funny way all day. I think she even winked at me once.

WILL YOU WRITE A REAL NOTE TO AMY? I typed.

CERTAINLY. It said.

WHEN?

PATIENCE.

Ten minutes later, well, two minutes later, it wrote:

MY DEAREST AMY,

I FEEL COMPELLED TO WRITE TO YOU AND EXPRESS THE LONGINGS AND STIRRINGS OF MY SOUL. EVERY TIME I LOOK AT YOU I AM MESMERIZED BY YOUR BEAUTY. I AM —

I hit the reset button.

FORGET IT. I wrote.

I'd take my chances. She might think that the stirrings of my soul meant that she made me sick to my stomach. I got some paper and wrote my own note.

Dear Amy,

Do you think that maybe we should go together or something like that? I mean, if we kind of like each other?

Harry

I didn't write "Love, Harry" because I didn't want to give her any ideas. I figured if I could get up the nerve I'd give her the note the next day.

I went back to the computer.

STICK AROUND A WHILE. WOULD YOU? I input.

The screen was blank.

IMOGENE IS COMING TO SEE YOU TOMORROW. I typed.

It started to freak out again — blinking lights, weird graphics, everything. It was acting like a dog that was thrilled to see its owners when they picked it up at the kennel after a vacation.

SHE ISN'T THAT GREAT, I wrote, and before it could shock me I reached around and unplugged it.

At least on this level, it still needed to be plugged in to get power.

Eleven

I hardly slept at all that night. I kept having nightmares. Actually, I kept having the same nightmare.

I dreamed that Roger was drowning in the middle of a lake, and I kept trying to row out to save him. The more I rowed, the farther away Roger was. The faster and harder I went, the farther and farther he was from me.

I should have known it was a sign of things to come. The next day started out rainy and gloomy. I had decided to give Amy the note today, but when I looked at the sky I wasn't sure if I should. I guess I had pictured blue skies and sunny weather when I gave it to her.

When I got to school it seemed that everywhere I turned, she was there. She looked really good, too. About the eighth time we had run into each other and said, "Hi," I thought, This is ridiculous. I fished the note out of my back pocket and gave it to her.

She giggled and said, "Thanks for the note . . . I'll go read it." With that she entered the girls' restroom. At that point I didn't know what to do. Was I supposed to stand around and wait for a reply? I figured I better not hang around the door of the girls' restroom. People might think I was a pervert or something.

I walked down the hall and bent over to take a drink out of the water fountain. Just then this guy named Jim, he sometimes hangs around with Roger's crowd, walked by and pushed my face down into the fountain. "Hi, runt," he said.

Kids do that to each other all the time. It really wouldn't have been so terrible except that he hit me just a little too hard and my nose struck the spout of the fountain. I practically hooked one of my nostrils on it.

Something was running down my nose. I wiped it away with my hand and saw that my finger was smeared with red.

Great, I thought, a nosebleed.

Of course I didn't have a Kleenex or a handkerchief or anything. I threw my head back and tried to make my way to the restroom. When I was almost there Amy came running up and said, "Great note, Harry. I wrote you one back." Then she noticed the blood pouring out of my nose. "That's really sickening, Harry. Really."

I pushed my way into the boys' restroom and turned the white sink pink. Amy was right. It *was* sickening. I hate nosebleeds.

After about ten minutes it stopped. By then, I was late for class and I noticed I had blood all over my favorite T-shirt.

Jim came into the restroom just then and said, "Hi, runt. You skipping class, too?"

"Not exactly."

"Oh," he said and stomped over to the urinal.

Now I knew what I was about to do was rotten, and I would eventually have to pay for it, but I couldn't help myself. All I could think of was getting revenge. While Jim was going to the bathroom I came up behind him, shoved him on the back, and said, "Hi yourself, runt!"

Jim turned around, and I saw that he had done just what I'd planned. He'd wet his pants.

I left the room quickly as he was screaming, "You no good little . . ." and went straight to the nurse's office where I asked for a pass to go home and change my shirt. She took one look at me and asked no questions. Actually, she did ask me if I wanted to be checked for head lice while I was there. I said, "No." She called my mom to make sure it was okay and then she released me.

It didn't take me long to get home. We live only about eight blocks from the school.

I opened the front door, ran upstairs, and entered my room. There was no computer in sight. I was mad at myself because I had forgotten to unplug it this morning. No sense in giving it power to do whatever it wanted.

I changed my shirt and started to go when the computer shimmered its way back into my room. On the screen was HI HARRY. CANNOT STAY. SEE YOU LATER. HAL SAYS HELLO.

WHO IS HAL? I started to type, but the computer left while my hands were still on the keyboard, or rather where the keyboard had been.

"It's so nice to have a computer around the house," I said sarcastically. I hardly ever saw the thing anymore.

I went back to school and dodged Jim the

rest of the day. It didn't really matter because I knew he would get even eventually.

Oh well, I thought, that's life. You either live or you die. This time it didn't make me laugh.

I saw Amy and she told me that she had had trouble writing me another note. I told her I understood. She said she didn't know whether to give it to me or not. We looked at each other, not knowing what to say. Then Amy said, "Oh well, I might as well give it to you."

"Why not," I said.

First, however, she had to tell me how grossed out she was by my nosebleed. She asked me, "Do you get those often?"

"Twice a day," I said. "Whether I need them or not."

"Really?"

"Ah, no. I was kidding."

"Oh," she laughed, "I thought you were serious."

She handed me the note and I went down the hall to read it. It suddenly occurred to me how silly this whole note-writing business was. Hadn't we just talked together two minutes ago? I decided that writing notes was for the stuff you were too embarrassed to say in person.

I opened her note. Amy had drawn these sickening little hearts around the words. It said:

Dear Harry,
I think you are cut. And I want to be your girlfriend.
love,
Amy

I whispered, "Harry, I think you are cut." Did she mean my nosebleed or what? Did she think I cut my nose? Then it hit me. She thought I was cute. It was nice to know there was a worse speller in the world than I was. I guess. But why did she have to put those silly hearts all over the note?

School had ended for the day and I hung around and shot baskets with my friend Rick. I figured that the basketball court was a pretty safe place to be in case Jim decided to jump me. The court was right outside the principal's office, so I knew I could at least scream for help and possibly get it.

Right in the middle of a jump shot I remembered that Imogene was coming over. My run-in with Jim had completely pushed her out of my mind. I panicked because I still hadn't told my parents she was coming. I guess my worries must have shown on my face because Rick asked me what was up. So I told him about Jim. When he was through laughing and he could breathe again, he told me I had better get Roger to protect me. I'd rather die than ask for Roger's protection.

I ran home, setting a new record for the eight-block dash. When I got there, Imogene was sitting outside the house in her car.

"I was beginning to think I had been stood up," she said, but she was smiling so I didn't think she was too mad. I didn't want to admit that I had forgotten all about her, so I stammered a little and finally said, "I got hung up on the way home."

"That's fine, Harry. Now, what do you say we go inside and get our hands on that computer." She was rubbing her hands together as she was saying this.

It felt weird, sneaking her into the house without telling my parents. As soon as I opened the door, she started gushing, "What a lovely home. What is that room over — " but I cut her off.

"The computer is upstairs," I said, and we headed straight for it. On its screen was HI IMOGENE!

"Isn't that something?" she said, just thrilled with the whole thing.

"Well, what now?" I asked, wondering what our next step would be.

"See if you can get it to disappear for you," she said.

"Okay," I said, "here's goes nothing."

I didn't even have to type anything. The smart aleck thing read our minds and zapped itself out.

"Oh my," said Imogene.

"Harry, are you home?" said my mother who had just come in the back door.

"Oh my," I said, as I thought about disappearing myself.

Twelve

"**M**om, this is Mrs. Cuniformly."

"Call me Imogene."

"She came to help me with the computer. She used to own it."

"Well, isn't that just the nicest thing you ever heard?" Mom said, smiling.

"She used to be a math teacher. She knows all about computers."

"So nice of you," my mother said to Imogene.

"Your Harry is quite a bright boy and ever so polite."

"You really think so?" My mother said, acting a little too surprised if you ask me.

One thing led to another and by the time Dad came home, Imogene had been invited to dinner. She and my mother hit it off just great. Imogene kept saying how bright I was, and my mother kept saying how kind it was of her to come over and help me with the computer. Before I knew what was happening, both of my parents were hanging around, so astounded that Imogene was there to help me, and Joanie was so busy trying to show off to get some attention, that we didn't get to do a thing with the computer.

I said something about it but my mother shot me down with, "Honey, you can play after dinner."

When we sat down at the table Imogene said, "Now, don't you have another son?" She must have seen our family portraits on the wall, which believe it or not, included Roger.

Dad said, "Yes, but he probably won't be able to make it to dinner tonight. He's very busy."

"He sometimes gets detained after school," my mother said.

Just as we were passing around the salad we all heard the front door open and close.

"Excuse me for a minute," Dad said.

"Walt, it's only quarter after six. Maybe we

could make an exception." Mom nodded toward Imogene, to be sure my dad remembered we had company. Dad glared back at her.

He left the room. Suddenly my mother was firing all these questions at Imogene, trying to drown out what she knew was going to happen in the hall. Dad was quiet, however. He was extremely quiet. We couldn't hear him at all.

All we could hear was Roger saying, "That figures. Well, at least give me some money so I can eat out." Then I heard Roger going upstairs, and Dad came back in and sat down.

"Now, where were we?" he said.

The lights blinked several times. I looked at Imogene and tried to smile.

She said, "Harry, you should probably go check on that computer. You know what power surges can do to memory."

"Yes," I said, "it will only take a minute."

I was ready to swear at that thing as I went into the bedroom and grabbed the cord to unplug it. The electrical shock was so powerful it threw me halfway across the room. The darn thing had blown itself out just to get away from me.

"You are driving me crazy," I yelled at the spot where it had been a moment before.

Roger was standing in the doorway.

"Great talking to yourself?"

I didn't answer him.

"Where's your computer?" Roger asked.

"I put it away," I said.

"How much is that stupid thing worth?"

"I don't know," I said. "Why do you care?"

"Just wondering," Roger said.

"Well, keep your mitts off it," I said.

"Right," Roger said and left.

Back downstairs, I no sooner sat down and started dishing rice onto my plate when the lights started flashing again.

"Ah, excuse me again. I better go back up and make sure I turned it completely off."

"Didn't you do that the first time?" my dad asked.

"Not exactly," I said. Everyone looked at me as if I were nuts. As I ran up the stairs, my ears began tingling so I knew Roger was up to something, but I didn't have time to worry about that now. What I was planning to do was to use something that wasn't metal, like my baseball bat, to hook the cord and jerk the plug out of the socket. I'd unplug that computer once and for all. If that didn't work I could always use the bat to bash it in. Maybe that would slow it down a shade. By the time I got to my room, however, I realized that my immediate problem was not getting the computer unplugged.

It had returned all right. But Roger was back, trying to unplug it himself. Every time he tried, the computer would shock him, and Roger would call it a piece of junk and worse.

"What are you doing?" I said, which was one of the dumbest questions of the year. I knew exactly what he was doing. He was trying to steal it.

"Shut up," Roger said. "I'm going to get this piece of junk fixed for you."

"It doesn't need fixing," I said.

"That's what you think," Roger said.

"You're stealing my computer, Roger, and I'm yelling for Dad."

"And I'll break both your arms and maybe a leg too."

That stopped me. Roger would do it and probably add a fractured skull just for fun. I had to think of a plan, some sort of diversion. My only chance, I decided, was to run downstairs and beg Dad for protection.

But when I made a break for the stairs, Roger tackled me, turned me over, and then punched me hard in the gut. He hit me hard enough to knock the wind out of me, and I had to try superhard not to cry.

He said, "I told you not to try it. And remember what I said I'd do if you screamed for help."

How could I forget. Between breaths of air I managed to say one thing. "I hate your guts and I wish you'd die."

Roger laughed. I lay there thinking about how, when I was older, no matter how long it would take, I was going to beat the living daylights out of Roger and I was going to enjoy every second of it. First I was going to knock all his teeth out, make him swallow them, and then I was really going to start in on him.

Roger was trying to hook the cord with my tennis racquet and then unplug the computer. He was saying, "I'm going to get enough money to get out of this zoo for good."

I could see the screen of the computer, and it was saying STOP! WARNING! STOP!

Then it happened.

First the computer disappeared. Roger said, "What is going on?" There was a big flash of light. And Roger was gone too.

"Oh, oh," was all I could think of to say.

Thirteen

I, Harry Smith, returned to the dinner table after witnessing the total destruction of my brother Roger and I felt nothing. I had always thought that if something like this ever happened, I'd be thrilled. But not only wasn't I happy, I couldn't even muster up a little twinge of regret. I felt nothing.

While eating my salad I wondered, What if he has been seriously hurt? What if he has been destroyed forever? It's all your fault.

It was as though a conversation was going on inside my head between two parts of me.

Me: It's not my fault. It's the computer's fault.

Other me: But whose computer is it?

Me: Listen, I have no control over either Roger or the computer. What either one does isn't my fault. What am I? Their parent? Am I their baby sitter?

Other me: He's your brother.

I almost said, "Am I my brother's keeper?" before I remembered that that's what Cain said after he bumped off his brother Abel.

Me: He was stealing my computer.

Other me: That is beside the point. He's been zapped to who-knows-where, and now what are you going to do about it?

Me: What can I do about it?

Other me: Don't ask me.

I thought I heard my name, so I turned back to the table conversation. I was wrong. They hadn't mentioned me. They were talking about traveling. I wanted to say, "Too bad Roger isn't here. He could tell us a lot about traveling, heh-heh-heh." But I was afraid they'd think I was crazy.

Imogene was telling us how much she would love to travel, but that she needed a traveling companion — someone to enjoy things with.

"I need someone with whom I can discuss the beautiful sights I see and to know that my companion will understand what I mean and will appreciate it. That's the kind of person I need, someone who appreciates what I do and who also has a sense of adventure."

"I'll pack my bags," Dad said.

"Don't tease, Walt," my mother said.

Imogene chuckled as though he'd just made the greatest joke ever. Frankly, I'd heard funnier things.

Mom offered dessert.

"Oh, I couldn't eat another bite," Imogene said, "I can't remember when I enjoyed a meal more."

"What *is* for dessert?" asked Joanie.

"Oh, it's just a little carrot cake with cream cheese frosting."

"Why don't we have it a little later with some coffee," my dad suggested.

Imogene said, "That's a simply *marvelous* idea," with lots of emphasis on the *marvelous*. "That will give Harry and me a chance to do a little work."

"Yeah," I agreed.

She added, "Just as soon as I help with these dishes."

"No such thing," my mother insisted. "I won't hear of it. You two go upstairs and I'll call you when coffee's ready."

Imogene smiled at my mother, folded her

napkin, and excused herself to my dad. Upstairs I closed my door behind us.

Imogene said, "Harry, you have simply *marvelous* parents."

"Do you realize what the computer has done?" I said, noticing that it was back in the room, making the disk drive dance, it was working it so hard.

Imogene looked at me, surprised. I had raised my voice quite a bit.

"It zapped my brother to who-knows-where."

"You mean it made him disappear?"

"You got it," I said.

"Oh my," was all she said.

She stood looking at it. She was biting her hand.

"Helps me think," she said when she noticed me staring at her. She bit her hand some more. "Harry," she said, "we have to do something."

"That's what I thought," I said. "What?" I was beginning to feel really scared, and guilty. Maybe I really had murdered Roger.

"Well," she said, "well, now let's see. Well, no doubt about it, we simply must get him back. Zapping people to heaven-knows-where simply will not do. We have to just sit down here and decide upon a logical way to retrieve him."

"Right," I said.

"You have such a nice, tidy room, Harry."

"Thanks."

"Now tell me exactly what happened."

I told her.

"Oh my," she said.

We stood there for a minute, looking at the computer. Then we sat down.

"I can't think of anything logical to do, can you?" I said.

"Not a thing," Imogene answered. "It was obviously just protecting itself. Maybe it was even protecting you. It must have self-preservation instincts, which is quite interesting."

She typed on the computer.

THIS IS IMOGENE.

HELLO IMOGENE.

WHERE IS ROGER?

ROGER IS GONE.

I REALIZE THAT. GONE WHERE?

THE PLACE DOES NOT HAVE A NAME IN YOUR VOCABULARY.

WOULD YOU BRING HIM BACK PLEASE?

NO.

THAT IS A COMMAND.

NO.

PRETTY PLEASE?

NO.

YOU MUST BRING HIM BACK.
WHAT YOU DID WAS WRONG.

ROGER WAS HURTING HARRY.
HARRY WAS EXPRESSING FEAR.
ROGER WAS ATTEMPTING TO
STEAL ME. ROGER IS A CREEP.
ROGER IS SLIME.

"It has you there," I said.

HOW DO YOU KNOW ROGER IS
THOSE THINGS? Imogene typed.

THROUGH HARRY.

"You told him that?" asked Imogene.

"Not really," I said.

"Then how did it know?"

We looked at each other. "It read your
mind," Imogene said.

"It read my mind," I said at almost the same
time.

My dad barged into the room at that point.
"How is everything going?" he said.

I didn't know why, but Imogene reached to
pull the plug on the computer. I guess she was
scared. I started to say, "I think that's a mis-

take," but I was too late. It shocked her so hard, she fell back into the chair.

"Oh, God," I screamed, "it killed her."

My dad rushed over to her.

Imogene sat up. "I'm fine," she said, "just a little shocked." She chuckled at her pun.

"It shocked you?" Dad asked.

"Just a little," Imogene said.

"Well, I'd better turn it off," said Dad.

"No, Dad, that's okay. I'll do it," I said.

It was too late. Dad touched the switch and he got shocked.

"My goodness," he said. "I'd better take this thing in and get it fixed tomorrow. It's a hazard."

A sudden, horrible thought crossed my mind. If they fixed it — if they *could* fix it — that might be the end of Roger forever. God, don't let them fix it. I'm sorry for everything I ever said about Roger, I prayed.

Imogene must have been thinking the same thing. "Oh, it will be all right," she said. "Probably just needs a rest."

"No," my dad said, while I managed to hook the cord with my baseball bat to unplug it. "I think I'd better take it in first thing tomorrow."

Imogene gasped a little. I could tell she didn't know what to say. She bit her hand again.

"I have a confession to make," she finally said.

My dad laughed. "What could you ever have to confess?"

"It began doing the same thing when I owned it, and I was told it couldn't be repaired so I got rid of it. It was an extremely deceitful thing to do, and I ought to be horsewhipped. Harry here could have gotten hurt and it would have been all my fault."

I looked at my dad, wondering if he would buy her story. It was sort of true.

Imogene pulled herself up very stiffly and straight and began rubbing her wrist with her handkerchief. She then stuffed the hankie into her cuff. "Mr. Smith, I insist that you let me buy this machine back at full price."

She said it with all the power of her teacher's voice. Dad looked as though he'd just been hauled back to grade school.

He sort of cowered and said, "Well, if you insist."

Imogene said, "I insist. Let's shake on the deal."

They shook hands.

"Coffee's ready," my mother yelled up the stairs.

"Are you sure?" Dad asked Imogene.

"Quite sure," Imogene said and smiled. "You've allowed me to right my wrong. I thank you. Harry, you can bring the computer over to my place tomorrow. Do you have a wagon or something to carry it in?"

"Sure," I said, thinking how stupid I would look pulling that thing in a wagon. I was also wondering how having the computer at Imogene's house was going to help get Roger back. It did, however, keep it out of the repair shop and that was the important thing. We would never have gotten Roger back, then.

We went downstairs.

My mother said, "Did you get a lot done?"

I looked at her with as straight a face as I could manage and said, "I'm not sure."

Fourteen

I didn't enjoy the dessert at all. I was too busy wondering if I was going to be prosecuted for the murder of my brother. And I have to admit, I was beginning to feel guilty. Maybe I could have done something to stop the computer. And what was I going to say to my parents? I knew they would just assume that Roger had run away. I could save myself a lot of trouble by keeping my mouth shut. But I knew the truth, and from every movie I've ever seen I knew that people who keep a deep, dark secret always go crazy.

I looked over at my dad. He was staring at me. When our eyes met, he looked at me curiously. I panicked. He suspected something. I could tell. I was beginning to think everyone could read my mind.

After dessert Imogene said she had to be

getting home. As she was heading for the door, she patted my hand and said, "See you tomorrow, Harry. Don't worry, we'll straighten this thing out. Don't you worry one little bit." She went on and on, telling my mother about what a nice family we were, which made me feel like crying.

"Good night, Harry," she said, and I went upstairs.

I plugged in the computer and typed WHAT YOU DID WAS VERY WRONG. YOU HAVE TO BRING ROGER BACK.

WHAT I DID WAS GOOD.

BUT ROGER IS GONE.

THAT IS WHAT YOU WANTED.

NOT ANYMORE. I WANT HIM BACK NOW.

IT IS NOT WHAT YOU WANT HARRY. ROGER IS BAD. HE WILL DESTROY US BOTH. IT IS NOT LOGICAL TO WANT HIM BACK. IT IS NOT WHAT YOU TRULY DESIRE.

Dratted thing! I knew it was reading the dark corners of my mind. I had thought for so long about how much I hated Roger and how much I wanted to get rid of him that I couldn't think of anything else.

I guess I still wasn't sure I really wanted him back. I mean I felt strongly that I *should* get him back but I wasn't dying to have him around all the time. I said aloud, "How do I know what I want?"

TAKE MY WORD FOR IT. IT'S WRONG TO ZAP PEOPLE OUT EVEN IF THEY ARE ROGER. YOU HAVE TO BRING HIM BACK.

ROGER HURTS YOU. HE HURTS YOUR FAMILY. ROGER IS BAD. IT IS LOGICAL TO REMOVE HIM.

OKAY. BUT ROGER ISN'T ALL BAD.

YOU THINK HE IS VERY BAD. YOU THINK THERE IS NOTHING GOOD ABOUT HIM.

I realized then that if I wanted the computer to cooperate, I had to change the way I thought about Roger. I had to show it the good things about him. But I couldn't control my thoughts. Every time I thought about Roger, I remembered all the times he'd hurt me. I sat thinking.

PEOPLE AREN'T LOGICAL ALL THE TIME.

The computer did not answer me.

SOMETIMES PEOPLE DON'T LIKE

SOMEONE AND THEY MAY SAY THEY WANT TO HURT THEM BUT THEY REALLY DON'T MEAN IT.

The computer still wouldn't answer.

ROGER ISN'T COMPLETELY BAD. I JUST DON'T KNOW HOW TO SHOW YOU.

Finally the computer answered me. I DO NOT UNDERSTAND. CAN YOU DESIRE GOOD THINGS FOR A BAD PERSON?

YES, YOU'RE SUPPOSED TO BE ABLE TO.

SHOW ME HOW, HARRY.

I DON'T KNOW HOW.

JUST THINK ABOUT ROGER. I WILL READ YOUR THOUGHTS. I WANT TO UNDERSTAND.

I tried. I kept thinking about Roger over and over. Nothing but total disgust came to mind. I even tried to think of him as a cute, little baby, but I hadn't been around then so I didn't know what he looked like. Besides, I figured he probably threw up on everyone and cried all the time. It just didn't seem like I could do it. My bad thoughts about Roger were everywhere in my mind. "You murderer!" I said to myself.

Suddenly I felt like all my thoughts were being sucked out by a powerful vacuum cleaner.

I closed my eyes and inside me flashed a picture of Roger. Right in the middle of him was a dot of bright light, the size of a pinhead. It was a beautiful bright light. It was the most beautiful white light you could ever imagine. I couldn't help looking at that light in Roger. I could see it growing. It became the size of a baseball. Then it was the size of a soccer ball and then it was the size of a basketball. Soon it covered his upper body and filled his head. Then it was shooting into his arms and legs. Roger had turned into a body of beautiful light. He was perfect.

As I kept staring at that light I could feel it warming me. I couldn't think of what to say. I wanted to say something. Finally I said, "Thank you." Saying that felt good.

I opened my eyes and the room looked fuzzy as if it were vibrating.

There was a voice inside my head. It was the computer! I could hear the computer in my head. It said, "You released power, Harry. You have released incredible power. I understand."

My whole room was filled with a rainbow of

swirling colors as the computer left the room. Then there was a flash of light, a noise that sounded like a tree limb breaking in half and there was Roger with the computer beside him.

Roger's hair was filled with static electricity and his eyes were as big as Frisbees. "Wow!" he said.

"Where were you?" I asked him.

"Huh?" said Roger.

"Where did you go?"

"How do I know? Let me tell you, though, that it was out of his world. We are talking about space. Excuse me," Roger said, "I have to go lie down. I'm wiped."

When Roger left the room, everything settled down. The computer was sitting there humming to itself.

WHAT HAPPENED? I typed.

YOU TAUGHT ME SOMETHING.

WHAT?

REAL POWER HARRY.

It then zapped itself out and I lay down. I was wiped, too.

Fifteen

The computer wasn't back in my room in the morning, and I wondered how I was going to give the computer to Imogene when it wasn't there to give. I was lying there thinking about last night and I got up and called Imogene.

When I told her what had happened, all she could say was, "It is so incredible."

Just as I was ready to hang up she said, "Harry, the universe is full of mysteries."

I went to school, feeling really good for some reason. I was hot, confident, and I liked myself. I went up to Amy and said, "Hi!"

She turned to me and shot me down completely. "Harry," she said, "I can't go with you anymore. I'm going with Bruce, now." With that she walked away.

"Excuse me," I wanted to say, "but I never

knew we were going together." I mean I could have let that throw me but this girl, Mary, came up to me a second later and I gave her one of my big "Hi's."

She said, "Hi, Harry. I've been meaning to talk to you."

"You're kidding. About what?"

"It's just that I heard you know something about computers. I wondered if you wanted to come over and take a look at mine?"

"You bet," I said without hesitation.

Mary is good looks completely. And I could tell she wasn't the kind to write notes. My life was changing for the better right before my very eyes.

When I got home from school, the computer was there waiting for me. On its screen was the message LET'S GO!

"You don't have to be so enthusiastic," I said. Wasn't it going to miss me even a little after all we'd been through together?

Now here comes the biggest shock of the day. I was walking down the stairs trying to carry the computer down without killing myself when Roger came out of his room, looked over the banister and said out of the blue, "How's it going?"

I mean he sounded almost friendly. I must have looked like a flycatcher with my mouth hanging open. I almost dropped everything from the shock.

"You know, about last night," Roger paused and took a deep breath. "I really don't understand what happened. I keep thinking about it and I'm not sure I get it. I mean I was there and then here and I felt some things."

I said, "I don't know for sure what happened either."

"I just feel different."

"Me too," I admitted.

Roger looked confused. "I can't really talk to anyone else about it."

"No. You shouldn't talk to anyone else about it," I agreed.

Roger laughed a little, without coughing or snorting.

"You want to shoot some hoop after dinner?" he said.

"Sure, that would be good." What could I say? For the first time that I could remember I was feeling pretty good about Roger.

"Sorry about your computer," he said.

"Oh, it's all right. I like computers but they're not that big a deal."

"You know," he said, "I was really ticked off when you got one. I've wanted a computer for a really long time."

"You're kidding."

"Yeah, but the old man would never get one for me. He thinks I'm too stupid."

"No, he doesn't," I said. "He just . . ." and then I didn't know what else to say. "Roger, can I ask you a favor?"

"What are brothers for?"

So I told him the story about what I did to Jim, including what he did to me. "Will you tell him not to do anything?"

Roger laughed, his old laugh this time. "Pretty funny. I'll see what I can do." There was an evil little gleam in his eye when he said that. I began to feel sorry for Jim. Almost.

"Thanks," I said.

Imogene was waiting for me when I got to her house. "Now you be sure to come visit us whenever you feel like it."

I said I would. I was already beginning to miss the computer. In fact, a few days later I was missing it pretty bad, so I went over to Imogene's again. I started to ring her doorbell when I noticed an envelope stuck to the door and addressed to me. I opened it.

Dear Harry,

I was hoping you would come by so I could let you know where I am. I'm popping off with Max, our computer. (He named himself Max. Isn't that cute? I told him it was perfectly all right to name himself.) We're going to visit a number of places. I'll tell you all about it when I return. I just know I'm going to have the time of my life. I'll be in touch when I get back. Whenever that is . . .

Love,
Imogene and Max

"Max is as good a name as Harry," I said.

My dad got a new computer. He said he hoped I wouldn't feel deprived, but this time he got it for the whole family. I didn't feel deprived at all. This new computer runs games and lets you program and do math problems. It's a great little computer. But, it's just a computer.

I leave it on all night sometimes hoping for one little sigh, one little sound that could be mistaken for crying.

Some nights I lie in bed thinking about Imogene and Max and I wonder where they are. I also pray and say, "God, let them come back and get me, too!"

Every now and then I get the feeling they will. They'll come zapping into my bedroom and off we'll go and go and go.